Buddy the Buzzbomber

W9-BTW-393

Copyright © 2012 by Matthew M. Douglas and Brandy Van Zalen of Monarch Communications, LLC, located at 7131 Oran SE, Cascade Woods, Michigan, 49546.

All rights reserved

Buddy the Buzzbomber and its illustrations are copyrighted property of Matthew M. Douglas and Brandy Van Zalen.

No portion of this book may be reproduced—mechanically, electronically, or by any other reproducing procedure currently used or yet to be devised, including information storage and retrieval systems—without written permission of the author, Matthew M. Douglas and illustrator, Brandy Van Zalen (except by a reviewer who may quote brief passages in a review).

Book Summary: Buddy the Buzzbomber is inquisitive, pugnacious, and annoying in a very cute way. In school, Buddy finds out he is a "bee mimic" who can see only during the day. His teacher warns him not to scare other creatures and not to fly at night. This is to no avail. After scaring a number of animals Buddy is coaxed into flying at night by a large night-flying hawkmoth, which leads to troubles only his parents can resolve.

Search Words: 1) Interracial family 2) Family unity 3) Be true to yourself 4) Nature education 5) Moth life cycle

Books published by Monarch Communications LLC are available at special discounts when purchased in bulk for premiums and sales promotions as well as for fundraising or educational use. Please contact Dr. Matthew Douglas at matt.thewriter@yahoo.com with any inquiries in this regard.

Printed in the United States of America

First Printing: November 2012
Second Printing: March 2013

ISBN: 978-0-9709646-9-4

Graphic Design:	Brandy Van Zalen
Cover/Illustrations:	Brandy Van Zalen
Printing Services:	Grand Rapids Community College, 143 Bostwick NE, Grand Rapids, Michigan, 49503
Scientific Photos:	http://thedrunkbirder.wordpress.com
Promotion:	Kendall College of Art and Design of Ferris State University

Dedicated to Buddy.

A pure Michigan summer was on its way! Bumblebees and butterflies were everywhere, and the fragrance of the early summer flowers hung ever-so-softly in the air. It made you feel good just to be alive! Enjoying the long spring day were two hummingbird hawkmoths, Marvin and Sarah, who looked like big bees as they hovered over a honeysuckle bush. (But they were moths!) Marvin was very dark and had brown eyes and Sarah was very light and had blue eyes. Together, they were inspecting a small silken cocoon.

"He was so small as a child," Sarah said, worried, "I don't know if he'll make it. But I thought I heard a squeak!"

Just then the door of the cocoon opened a bit and a bright fuzzy head appeared. Marvin and Sarah hovered even closer to get a good view. The child had a tan face with wild springy hair that made lots of crazy curls.

Suddenly the rest of the cocoon exploded into a million pieces and a tiny missile-like creature flew straight up in a blur!

"What was that?" shouted Sarah. "I'm not sure!" said Marvin dumbfounded. "Wait! Oh my gosh! He's…he's a…" "What?" said Sarah anxiously, waiting for Marvin to hurry up and finish his sentence.

"He's a *buzzbomber*!" his father said in awe, craning his neck as their newborn son flew like a banshee around them. "I always wanted a buzzbomber son!" said Marvin.

Then the young boy slowed down and hovered directly over Marvin and Sarah: "Hi you guys!" he shouted in a very tiny voice. "Are you my parents?"

"Yes!" Sarah shouted back. "Your name shall be Buddy!"

"Ohhhh!" he said, with an upside-down smile.

With that Sarah and Marvin flew up to greet Buddy. "Buddy, you must come down now and rest so that your wings can harden!" Marvin said. "They are still soft and you are very young!"

"And what about your tongue?" his mother admonished. "You've got to put that together before you do anything else!" With a frown Buddy descended, landing softly on a leaf of viburnum, exposing his thorax to the sunshine.

"And you'll use too much energy flying like that," Marvin warned. "Save that for buzzing flowers when you want nectar and pollen."

"That doesn't sound like much fun," Buddy responded. "I really like buzzing as high as I can go!"

"Well, there are a few things you must learn first," Sarah said gently, putting a few hands on Buddy's face. "First, let me show you how to put your tongue parts together to make a *proboscis*. Watch carefully, because your proboscis is very, very long!"

Buddy practiced coiling and uncoiling his new proboscis until finally he got it right.

"Perfect!" said his parents together. "You can start school tomorrow!"

"School?" asked Buddy, "What is that? I just got here!"

The next day, the family woke up from beneath the honeysuckle leaves and stretched together.

"Good morning, Buddy! Are you ready for school?" his mother asked sweetly.

After a breakfast of honeysuckle nectar, Buddy followed his parents to Bumblebee Hawkmoth Elementary. Children were busy playing outside on a nearby swing set, and when Buddy flew up to say "hello," one looked up and shouted "BEE!"

With that, they all took off screaming at the top of their lungs. Buddy was very hurt and pouted.

"I don't get it," Buddy said sadly. "Don't worry," his father said, "they are just humans. Sometimes they are very afraid of Nature." He buzzed his wings a bit and hovered over Buddy. "Anyway, you'll find out all about them today at school!"

Marvin introduced Buddy to Dr. Bombus, an elderly hawkmoth who opened the door: "Welcome!" he boomed in a deep voice. Buddy entered the classroom, perhaps a wee bit cocky.

"Sit down, please," Dr. Bombus said sternly. "We only have school for one day, so there is no time to waste! Tuck in your wings and roll up your proboscis!"

There were a number of new bumblebee hawkmoths there, all bright-eyed and eager to learn, except Buddy, who was rolling and unrolling his proboscis, absent-mindedly.

"Young man, what is your name?" Dr. Bombus asked in a huff of indignation. "Buddy…I think," he said. "Well, Buddy," Dr. Bombus said, "in this class you must put your proboscis away and concentrate on my lessons!" Buddy sheepishly coiled his tongue and looked at the floor. "And sit up straight please!" Dr. Bombus admonished.

"First," Dr. Bombus announced with a very officious voice, "this is you! You are a bumblebee hawkmoth, perhaps the most unusual of all insects. Why you ask? Because you look almost exactly like a bumblebee! So what you ask? Because furry animals and humans are afraid of bees! And you look like bees even when you fly! So you get protection because of the way you look!"

He adjusted his wire-rim glasses and looked over the students' blank faces. The class just sat there, staring into space, rolling and unrolling their tongues.

"Don't you get it?" Dr. Bombus asked impatiently, buzzing his wings to get their attention. "Big animals will be afraid of you, even though there is nothing to fear. You are harmless!! However, never *ever* pretend to be a bee!! Don't ever pretend to be something you are not! And never *ever* fly at night! Your eyes are different than other hawkmoths and you can't see at night!"

But Buddy wasn't listening. Instead, a big daydreamy grin spread over his face. "I'm a *buzzbomber!*" he said quietly under his breath. "*And everyone will be afraid of me!*"

Late in the afternoon the door to the schoolhouse opened. All the new bumblebee hawkmoths flew out in a rush, tumbling over one another. Buddy's parents waited anxiously for him to fly over.

"Buddy, come here—I'll show you how to sip nectar at flowers!" Buddy flew over with a sleepy yawn. "Like this!" his father said: "Hover first by making figure-8 sweeps with your wings. Next, roll out your tongue and get closer to the flower. Then, put your first two hands on the petals of the flower and steady yourself. But, keep buzzing so the nectar and pollen mixes really good! Now you can suck it up for energy! The pump muscles of your tongue will get bigger and stronger as you get older."

Buddy did exactly as his father said, zipping from flower to flower, unrolling and rolling his tongue, touching his hands gently to the petals as he sipped nectar. But after the tenth flower, Buddy spotted a wiener dog. A mischievous look spread across his face. Zoom! He buzzbombed the dog, back-and-forth, until it ran away barking. It finally hid under the porch. Buddy was proud of his new power and flew high in the air to celebrate.

Then Buddy spotted a doe and her fawn grazing peacefully by the little pond. Zoom! He buzzbombed them up-and-down, flying right in front of their eyes and noses. The deer bleated and scattered as fast as they could, kicking up their hooves high into the air.

Buddy was so excited!

A moment later Buddy spotted a very tired-looking Monarch butterfly with a tiny pink backpack flying overhead. Buddy flew directly at her, buzzing loudly. But this was no ordinary Monarch. She had been around the block a few times! Buddy got too close and she hit him with the edge of her forewing— right across his antennae! That smarted and sent him plummeting down toward the ground.

He crashed into a big flower—right into a gob of tumbling flower beetles busy nectaring. Buddy saw the look of fear in their faces and started to buzz loudly again. The beetles were so frightened they tumbled off the flower, scattering helter skelter. When they looked up they saw that Buddy was an imposter. They were furious!

Then, out of the corner of his eyes, Buddy saw what appeared to be many dark black bumblebee hawkmoths flying into holes in the deck. He zoomed over to buzzbomb them. Instead he was greeted by angry carpenter bees who instantly recognized him as a phony. They chased after Buddy, buzzbombing him instead! "Imposter!" they screamed. "You don't even have a stinger! But we do...*SEE!* So don't come back!"

Buddy flew high into the sky and turned around to look at his abdomen. He had nothing there except a tail that he could sometimes make into a fan. Disappointed and far from his parents he flew sluggishly near another honeysuckle bush. The sun was nearly setting. He hovered silently with a sad face and finally landed softly on a leaf.

"PSST," said something deep inside the bush. Buddy was scared but curious. He pushed back some leaves. There, hanging on a branch was a huge moth that looked exactly like him in shape! The moth was unrolling and rolling up his tongue—it was almost five inches long!

"Come here, son!" said the moth in a very deep voice. Buddy cautiously crawled closer. "Don't be afraid," said the moth, "I'm a hawkmoth just like you, only I can fly at night! Can you do that?"

"Well," Buddy said slowly, "my teacher said I should only fly in the daytime so I would get protection from the bumblebees flying at the same time. And he said my eyes are different and I won't be able to see well at night at all! Plus my bedtime is when the sun goes down." Buddy looked sheepishly at his feet.

"Ha!" exclaimed the moth. "So what does your teacher know? Are you afraid of having fun? The whole world is full of excitement at night! Frogs are croaking, owls are hooting, and bats are whizzing by—while you sleep! It's so much fun to tease them and drive them crazy because you can fly so much faster than they can!" He paused for a second and then looked Buddy straight in the eye: "Say, do you want to fly with me tonight? I'll help you and stick close to you so you don't get scared!"

Buddy thought for a moment. The sun was dropping from the sky like a stone and darkness was beginning to cover the land. In the shadow of sunset this huge moth looked big enough to protect him, so Buddy said, "Sure! I'm not afraid!"

"Good, good!" said the big moth. "You're not much of a hawkmoth if you can't fly at night!" he said with a wink.

In a distant part of the field, Buddy's parents were anxiously calling his name. But darkness came, and they couldn't see well enough to fly and search for Buddy. Sarah and Marvin huddled together, very worried. "We'll have to look again first thing in the morning," Marvin said sadly.

$\mathcal{A}$ moment later, the big moth began to vibrate his wings. The entire bush shook! "What are you doing?" Buddy asked. "Warming up!" said the big moth, breathing heavily. "You better do the same! Start vibrating your wings—but don't fly. Just shiver your muscles…you'll be amazed at how warm you'll get!" he said with a sideways smile at Buddy.

Buddy vibrated his wings and to his complete surprise, his body got warm—very warm! The huge hawkmoth smiled and then lifted off like a helicopter, wings humming with a low buzzing sound. Buddy was impressed and tried to follow, but it was very dark and the only bright spot in the sky was a full moon.

"Over here!" shouted the big moth. Buddy tried to follow his voice, but he couldn't see well and so he flew toward the moon instead. Then the loud droning sound of the big moth faded away in the darkness.

Buddy was very alone. And he was very scared!

Just then, when Buddy was as high as the tops of the white pines, an enormous shape flew just inches away from his face. It was a huge Black Witch moth, tired and cranky because he was migrating up from Texas. "Watch where you're going, twerp!" he shouted at Buddy. "You know you aren't suppose to fly at night! Where are your parents?" Buddy was ashamed. Why hadn't he listened to his parents and teachers?

As he flew higher, the air got colder, and Buddy was chilled. He remembered his teacher telling him that small moths lose heat quickly but big moths could fly into the cold of night. His wingbeats slowed and he felt wobbly. Then he saw what could only be called a nightmare: a *bat*!

From a distance it looked a lot like the big hawkmoth, but it had beady eyes and didn't look very friendly. Buddy got a bad feeling from the yellow glow in the bat's eyes.

A moment later the bat found Buddy with his sonar and wheeled around in the sky, diving directly at him. The clicking sound coming from the bat hurt Buddy's head and made him even dizzier. Fortunately, he could see the bat because the moon was behind it. As the bat got closer, Buddy froze with fear and started to fall from the sky.

And just in time! The bat opened its wings to catch Buddy in midair but just nicked his head instead! Now, Buddy was falling head-over-heels. Flashes of the moon were followed by flashes of dark. It was all so confusing, tumbling into the night!

Buddy fluttered his wings, and then fell. He fluttered his wings again, and then fell some more. Finally, he spotted what he thought was a patch of smooth light below him. It was the light of the moon reflecting from the big pond by his home! He tried to steer, but crash landed onto a large lily pad. Flat on his back, his little wings still whirring, Buddy slowly righted himself. But he was so cold!

Buddy got up on his wobbly legs and looked around. In the dim light he could make out the edge of the lily pad and then the reflecting eyes of huge creatures all around him: *frogs*! A big fat one hopped close, landing with a loud splat. Then its tongue flipped out from the rear of its mouth and grazed the fuzzy hair on the top of Buddy's head. Buddy stumbled backward into the water.

There he lay, flat on his back. He struggled to flap his wings, but they seemed stuck to the water. The frogs got closer and closer—all their eyes were on Buddy! He closed his eyes and prayed like there was no tomorrow.

Just then a huge animal erupted from the water below Buddy and pushed him onto the shore of the pond. A water snake had swallowed the frog!

The snake burped and said, "Say, aren't you a bumblebee hawkmoth?" "Yes," came Buddy's weak reply. "You're not supposed to fly at night, are you?" the snake asked. "No, I'm not," Buddy cried, "and I wish I had listened to my parents and teacher! They told me not to, but the big hawkmoth said it would be fun!"

"Well," the snake said, "your big friend the hawkmoth was eaten by a huge bullfrog just before you fell out of the sky! Maybe you should listen next time, huh?"

"Yes!" Buddy cried. "I promise I will listen!"

"Well, that's how it goes around here, ya know. You gotta pay attention, son! And you should never pretend to be someone you are not, because you are who you are and you can't change that for anybody. You must be true to yourself!" He smiled a fangy smile, but it did not scare Buddy at all.

"What should I do now?" Buddy asked the water snake. "Crawl up on that stick and fold your wings back so no enemies can see you," said the snake, "and then stay very still until the sun comes up. Your parents will find you in the morning. I'll bet they are sick with worry!"

Exhausted, cold, and unable to shiver any more to stay warm, Buddy climbed up the stick and fell into a deep sleep, hanging by his hands. His long antennae draped limply by the side of his wings.

The next morning the sun rose just as a large warty toad spotted Buddy stretching his wings. The stealthy toad set his sights on him and approached carefully, sneaking up from behind, not wanting to get stung! Buddy was still cold but tried to buzz his wings in a warning to the toad. The toad looked closer and then smiled: "Hey…you aren't a bee! You're a moth! I can tell by your long antennae!" The toad got ready to attack, but in the distance two figures were rapidly approaching.

They were Buddy's parents! "Fly, Buddy, fly!" shouted his father. Buddy started to buzz but he couldn't fly yet. He was still too cold.

"Watch me Buddy!" his father shouted. "I'll show you what a real buzzbomber can do!" With that, his father buzzbombed the toad over and over and over until it finally fell backward into the pond. Once again a huge splash broke the water as the snake's head appeared with a big smile. "Thanks little Buddy!" he shouted, not knowing that Buddy was Buddy's real name!

Buddy's mother came over and stroked the fuzz on his head with her wing. "And that's why we should always listen to our parents and teachers!" she said gently. "Save all the buzzbombing for your dad for now." And she smiled and hugged him closely.

"I promise, I promise!" said Buddy, shivering his wings. "Will you guys go drink nectar with me?"

"Of course!" they both said together, smiling. "That's what buzzbomber families do!"

Bumblebee Hawkmoth (*Hemaris thysbe*)

Bumblebee hawkmoths (also called hummingbird moths) are found throughout the northern areas of the world. There are perhaps 20 species of these incredibly fascinating insects, all of which hover like small hummingbirds but look like large bumblebees. They are so strikingly like these creatures in flight that they are often mistaken for them.

The adults described in *Buddy the Buzzbomber* are much larger than other members of the genus *Hemaris*. Many people have seen them but few probably realized they are moths! You can tell by looking for the large, almost clubbed antennae as they hover, and the peculiar fantail at the end of their abdomen (shown only once in this book since Buddy is obviously a cartoon of the real thing).

There is some variability, both seasonal and geographic, in the genus *Hemaris*, and there may be a number of cryptic or "hidden" species that look like them and are difficult to tell apart. There is so much we just don't know! *Hemaris thysbe*, the species of bumblebee hawkmoth described in *Buddy the Buzzbomber*, is found from the South to the Rocky Mountains and through much of Canada and most of eastern Alaska. Throughout its range it typically prefers the edges of hardwood forest and their adjacent meadows and clearings. However, it is a very common moth in the suburbs as well, especially if open areas are available with lots of nectar resources, including nectar-bearing cultivated plants such as *Verbena*, *Lantana*, and *Buddleja* (butterfly bush), which they particularly like.

Unlike most other members of the family Sphingidae (sphinx moths) to which *Hemaris* belongs, the bumblebee hawkmoths have light-adapted eyes and therefore can only see during the daylight hours. The larger sphinx moths, including some tropical species with 10-inch wingspans and bodies that weigh as much as small birds, have dark-adapted eyes and can only fly at night. Research shows that small bumblebee hawkmoths such as *Hemaris* can fly without overheating during the daytime, but large hawkmoths will quickly overheat and therefore can only fly during the cooler night periods. This may be the reason that some small hawkmoths adapted themselves to daytime flight.

It may seem strange, but the wings are completely covered with scales when the adults emerge from the pupa. With the first flight, however, after the wings have hardened, the scales in the middle of the wings are shed, making the wings appear transparent there. This bizarre characteristic, coupled with the unusual daytime flight of the adults, is what makes them appear like bees or hummingbirds.

When a hummingbird hawkmoth is captured, even by hand, it makes a wild buzzing sound just like a bee and may curl up its abdomen as if to sting you. But this is all just a hoax. You can tell it's a moth by looking at the antennae—they are very long compared to those of a bumblebee.

There are at least two, sometimes three broods of these fascinating insects every year, except for the more northern areas of North America. Eggs are laid singly on the underside of the leaves of the host plant (viburnum, honeysuckle, blueberries and cranberries are favorites, although there are others). The caterpillars are sluggish feeders, and are often found resting on the midvein of the leaf during the day. When a larva is ready to molt into the pupa, it first spins a sturdy cocoon of silk and debris. The last brood of the summer or fall overwinters and emerges as moths in the spring.